APPL

WITHDRAWN

The Adventures of Sam X

MASTER OF THE WEATHER

by Hubert Ben Kemoun

illustrated by Thomas Ehretsmann
translated by Genevieve Chamberland

Librarian Reviewer
Marci Peschke
Librarian, Dallas Independent School District
MA Education Reading Specialist, Stephen F. Austin State University
Learning Resources Endorsement, Texas Women's University

Reading Consultant
Elizabeth Stedem
Educator/Consultant, Colorado Springs, CO
MA in Elementary Education, University of Denver, CO

STONE ARCH BOOKS
MINNEAPOLIS   SAN DIEGO

First published in the United States in 2008
by Stone Arch Books,
151 Good Counsel Drive, P.O. Box 669
Mankato, Minnesota 56002
www.stonearchbooks.com

Library of Congress Cataloging-in-Publication Data
Ben Kemoun, Hubert, 1958–
    [Maître du temps. English]
    Master of the Weather / by Hubert Ben Kemoun; translated by
Genevieve Chamberland; illustrated by Thomas Ehretsmann.
    p. cm. — (Pathway Books Editions / The Adventures of Sam X)
    ISBN 978-1-4342-0479-0 (library binding)
    ISBN 978-1-4342-0529-2 (paperback)
    [1. Fantasy games—Fiction. 2. Weather—Fiction. 3. Magic—
Fiction.] I. Chamberland, Genevieve. II. Ehretsmann, Thomas, ill.
III. Title.
PZ7.B4248Mas 2008
[Fic]—dc22   2007030731

Summary: Sam and all of his friends love *Terror Universe* trading cards.
Sam trades a galactic soldier card to Gavin and receives some interesting
cloud cards in return. When the cloud cards are played, they change the
weather. During a blizzard, one of the cards is lost. The weather cannot
change, and Sam and Lionel must search for the card.

Art Director: Heather Kindseth
Graphic Designer: Kay Fraser

1 2 3 4 5 6 13 12 11 10 09 08

Printed in the United States of America

TABLE OF CONTENTS

Chapter 1

COOL CARDS

All of my friends were crazy about trading cards. Especially the cards for the Terror Universe game. Everyone I knew had some. We traded them at school, usually during lunch when the teachers weren't looking.

Lionel and I spent most of our allowances on them. We bought some new cards every week, but I got my best cards through trades.

Each card in the Terror
Universe game was
different. Some of them
had pictures showing
soldiers from different
planets. Other cards
had fighting weapons or
strange monsters.

It was pretty easy to
play the game, if you knew
what you were doing.

Each player picked up
a card from his pack. Then
he had to play it against a
card someone else had. We
created huge battles with
our cards. The battles could
last for days!

One day after school,
a bunch of us were trading
cards, like we always did.

It was a nice afternoon,
but I noticed that the sky
was full of strange clouds.

Gavin really wanted
one of my soldier cards.
"I'll trade a laser for your
galactic musketeer," he said.

"No way. That's not good
enough," I said.

I put my cards behind
my back. I was very tough
when I made my trades. I
wasn't going to let someone
get any of my good cards.

"Listen, Sam, I lost a lot of my cards last week, and I really need a soldier," Gavin whined. "Come on."

He looked through his cards. Then he looked up. "Here! I'll add an iron sword!" he said.

"I have tons of swords," I said.

Gavin sighed. Just then, the wind blew some cards out of his hands. They fluttered onto the ground. I had never seen cards like those before. Each of them had a different kind of cloud on it.

"What are those?" I asked.

Gavin shrugged. "I don't know how to use them," he admitted. "I think they change the weather in the game."

I frowned. "I don't get it," I said. "What's the point?"

"I don't really know," Gavin said. "I think it has something to do with slowing down your enemies, by sending a rainstorm or snow." Then Gavin's face lit up. He said, "I'll give you all of them for your galactic soldier."

My best friend, Lionel, was examining the cards closely. "Where did you get these?" he asked.

"I traded with my neighbor last week. I gave him an invisibility card for them," Gavin told us.

"Your neighbor?" Lionel snorted. "He's some old guy. He doesn't know anything about Terror Universe!"

Gavin rolled his eyes. "So, Sam, are you trading or not?" he asked me.

I thought about it. I knew Gavin wasn't going to add anything else to the trade.

Finally, I said, "Okay, it's a deal."

I handed my galactic soldier to Gavin, and he handed me a stack of cards.

On the way home, Lionel was laughing. "That was a pretty good trade," he told me. "But you're dreaming if you think your little weather cards can stop my soldiers and my weapons."

I shrugged my shoulders. "Whatever," I said.

Lionel always thought he could beat me, even though I was really good at Terror Universe.

"Anyway, I don't need my new cards to squish you," I said. "Even without the weather cards, I could destroy your army!"

Lionel laughed again. "Who are you kidding?" he said. "No way."

"Just wait! Tomorrow's game will prove it," I told him.

Lionel said, "Yeah, but I'll be the winner!"

I snorted. "You are so funny sometimes!" I told him.

We were in front of Lionel's house. I could see his mom through the window.

She waved at me. I waved back.

"See you tomorrow, future loser!" Lionel said.

"See you tomorrow, already loser!" I said back.

Chapter 2

THE STORM

The next afternoon, Lionel and I were sitting on the floor in my bedroom. There was a half circle of cards between us.

We were in the middle of a long battle. Our armies were marching in the desert. I had already fought off Lionel's planes with my bombers.

We had been playing for an hour and I was doing great! My army was strong.

All of a sudden, my luck changed. I was hoping to pull out a sunset card so I could attack Lionel's camp at dark and scatter his army. For some reason, I kept picking up the wrong cards.

On the other hand, Lionel started having good luck. He kept getting cards that could defeat my army.

That meant I had to defend my camp more and more. My army was doomed.

I was getting desperate. I needed a weapon, and I needed it fast.

It was my turn. I stared down at my pile of cards. Then I picked up a card, but it wasn't the weapon card I wanted. It was one of the cloud cards I had won in my trade with Gavin. The card had the word *cumulonimbus* printed on it.

"Oh, man!" I yelled.

Lionel laughed. "I bet you were hoping you'd get a weapon, weren't you?" he said. He had figured out my strategy.

"Oh well, you won't get it, and you're going to lose!" he added, smiling.

I hate losing. And now Lionel was really starting to get on my nerves!

"Don't get too excited yet," I told him, smiling. "Things are changing. I will turn your soldiers' armor into rust with rain from this cloud!"

Lionel laughed again. "Oh no, I'm so scared!" he joked.

I placed the strange cloud card on the carpet. Then it was Lionel's turn to pick a card.

Before drawing his card, he looked carefully at my cloud card. Then he glanced out the window.

He said, "That's funny. Your card looks just like the clouds outside. It was nice out when I got here. It's weird how the weather changes so fast."

I looked out the window. Lionel was right. The sky was filled with clouds.

Just then, it started to rain. "Oh great!" I said.

I was disappointed. I had planned to go skateboarding later.

I sighed and looked at Lionel. "So, are you playing?" I asked.

Lionel nodded. He reached down and drew a dragon fire card. Then he played it against my soldiers and tanks. They all burned up.

It was my turn. I was just about to draw a card. Then I heard some weird noises outside.

"What's going on?" asked Lionel, standing up.

We ran to the window and looked out.

It was amazing! Hail as big as quarters was dropping from the sky. It was bouncing off the cars parked on the street.

Then it started to thunder. We could see lightning off in the distance.

People outside were running around. They were trying to find shelter from the rain and hail.

Long lines of cars were slowing down in the street. The street was already almost covered in big, white chunks of icy hail.

"This weather is totally crazy!" Lionel whispered.

I let my eyes drift over to our cards. I noticed the weird cloud card I had won from Gavin.

"Yeah, it is" I said. "Too crazy."

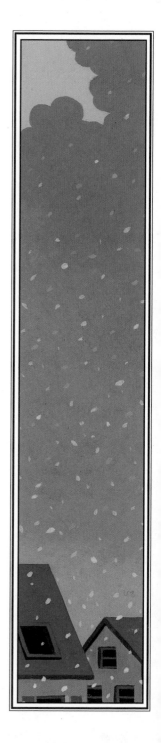

Lionel rolled his eyes. "It's not like this is the first storm that ever happened in June, Sam!" he said.

"I know," I told him. "That's not what the weird thing is. Look!" I picked up the *cumulonimbus* card from the pile and showed it to him. "Read it!" I said.

Lionel rolled his eyes again and read the tiny words that were printed on the card. "'This card brings rain, storms, and sometimes hail,'" he read out loud.

Then he looked up at me and shook his head. "It's just a game, Sam. It didn't cause the storm," he told me.

The weather forecast on TV that morning had said it was supposed to be sunny and dry all day. Wow, he was really wrong about that!

"The weatherman said there was no chance of storms," I told Lionel. "No chance at all."

Lionel laughed and turned away from the window. "The weatherman is wrong all the time," he said. "Come on, let's keep playing!"

But I had an idea. "Hold on. I want to check something," I said. "Don't worry, I'm not going to cheat."

I looked through my pile of cards. I wanted to find another one of the cloud cards that I had gotten from Gavin.

I found a card that said *cirrus*. It showed a picture of a small, curly cloud. I placed the card on the carpet.

Then I returned to the window. I stood next to Lionel.

Lionel's eyes got wide. "This is so strange!" he whispered. "It stopped!"

The sky was changing right in front of our eyes. New clouds, just like the one in the picture on the new card, were taking over the sky.

The storm stopped. The sun was coming out.

"This is not a coincidence," I said. "The weather doesn't change this fast!"

Lionel looked at me. He looked a little scared.

"Those cards," he whispered. "Where did they come from?"

Chapter 3

SUMMER SNOWBALLS

"A severe hailstorm rolled over the area today. There were several reports of hail as big as ping-pong balls! Damage was widespread," the news reporter said.

Lionel and I were lying on the floor in the living room, watching TV.

The TV news showed pictures of damaged houses, trees, and cars. Then the TV showed a farmer, who was being interviewed.

"It was a monster storm. It came in a flash! We had no warning at all," the farmer said.

Then the TV showed some damaged roofs close to my house. Two chimneys had fallen down, but luckily, no one had been hurt.

"Our city suffered a strange attack from bad weather this afternoon. Not one of the weather reporters saw this coming!" said another reporter. Then he added, "Tomorrow, the forecast calls for lots of sunshine!"

Sunshine, huh? We'll see, I thought.

"This is so weird," my mom said. "Global warming is changing everything."

Lionel and I quickly grabbed a bite to eat. We had some chicken and a bag of chips. Then we went back to my bedroom to continue our game.

It was Lionel's turn. But before he chose another card, he asked, "Do you really think we caused all of that?"

"Of course we did," I whispered. "You know it as well as I do!"

We went on with our game, but we played slower and more carefully than normal. I think we were both worried about what might happen if we picked up the wrong card.

Outside, the sky was bright blue. There wasn't a single cloud. The sun was shining brightly.

It was a perfect afternoon.

Summer didn't officially start for another two weeks, but it felt like summer had already begun.

When it was my turn, I drew another one of the cloud cards from the pile.

The card showed fluffy little clouds that looked like white sheep in a blue prairie. So far, so good.

"These look like nice clouds!" I said, showing Lionel the card.

"Don't tell me you're going to make hail fall again," Lionel said.

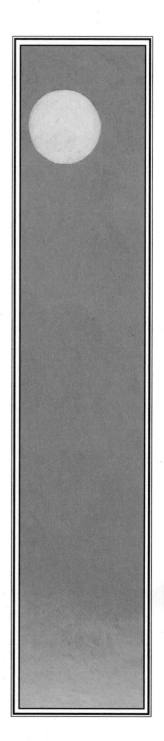

I examined the card, which said *altocumulus*. "I don't think so," I said. "It says these clouds don't cause rain or snow. Should I try it?"

"If I say no, will that stop you?" asked Lionel with a nervous laugh.

"No," I said.

I placed the *altocumulus* card on the floor. Then we ran over to my bedroom window.

Within seconds, the sky became crowded with a herd of fluffy clouds. A breeze gently pushed them over the river. They did look like little sheep.

"This is totally crazy!" Lionel said. He kept rubbing his eyes, and then looking back at the sky. He couldn't believe what he was seeing.

I was excited. "I am the Master of Weather!" I shouted. "This is so cool!"

"Let me try!" Lionel yelled.

"Go ahead! There are more clouds in the pile," I said, still excited.

Lionel sat down. He picked up my stack of cards and started to look through it.

Then he looked up and asked, "Sam, have you ever been skiing or gone sledding or snowboarding?"

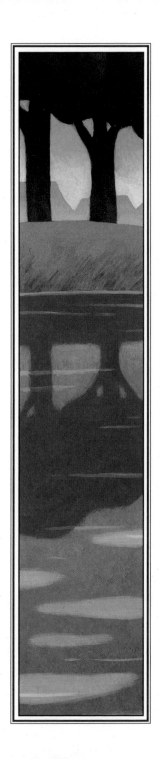

"No," I answered. "My mom always promised that we would go to the mountains someday, but we never have."

I stopped quickly. Suddenly, I realized why Lionel had asked me that question.

He waved a card at me. I read the word *nimbostratus* printed on it.

"Will you let me borrow a sweater and some gloves?" Lionel asked. "Do you have an extra pair of boots?" A sly grin crept over his face.

"What are you going to do?" I asked.

"Watch this!" Lionel yelled. "Snow in the middle of June. This will be great!"

He placed the card on top of the other cards in our game. We waited.

At first, nothing happened. The sun was still bright. I started to think that it wasn't going to work.

Then Lionel pointed outside. I could see dark and thick gray clouds coming in. They were coming closer, slowly at first. Then they quickly covered the sky.

Soon, the neighborhood was wrapped in cold darkness. Snowflakes started to fall.

The first flakes were little. They melted before they even touched the street.

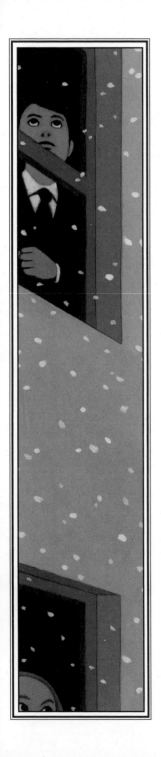

But soon, the snowflakes got bigger and heavier. Within half an hour, the roofs, the streets, and the river were covered in white!

Lionel and I quickly put on sweaters and went outside. Once we were out in the snow, we stuck our tongues out to catch the flakes.

The snow was cold on my tongue. It was weird, but I loved it.

I had never seen so much snow before.

Lionel and I started a snowball fight. I wanted to roll in the snow, but throwing snowballs was just as fun.

People stared out at us through their windows, wondering what was going on.

Chapter 4

THE WEATHER MASTERS

We were completely wet and cold. But Lionel and I had fun!

Our snowball fight was in the middle of the parking lot. More kids from the block joined us, but they all went home after only a few minutes. I guess they were too cold.

After a while, Lionel and I got bored with our game. Then we started making a snowman.

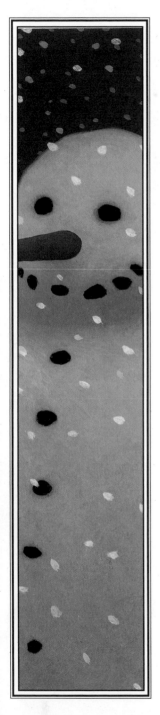

Soon, it was night. The snow was still falling. It came down harder than it had during the day.

The wind blew the snow across the ground and into our frozen faces. We were really cold, but we didn't go in. Lionel and I wanted to finish our snowman before we went back inside. It didn't take long.

Once we were done, Lionel found a stick and wrote in the snow: LIONEL AND SAM.

I added: THE MASTERS OF WEATHER.

Then Lionel turned to me. "This is awesome, but it's getting too cold. Let's go back inside," he said. He was shivering.

I was thinking the same thing. My teeth were chattering.

Then the wind became ten times worse. The icy blasts blew straight at us as we walked back to my apartment building.

We trudged toward the door. Before long, I couldn't even see Lionel.

"Where are you?" I yelled.

There was no answer. The wind just blew harder.

I could barely see the lights from the apartment windows. They seemed so far away. The snow and wind kept pushing me back. My hands and face were turning numb.

I couldn't even stand anymore. I fell, exhausted, onto the ground only a few feet from the door.

Then Lionel appeared out of the snow. "It's all right!" he yelled over the wind. "Come on. It's warm inside."

Lionel had to carry me up the hall. Inside, he helped me get into the elevator.

It was warm inside. I thought we were safe.

But as soon as I opened the door to my apartment, a freezing cold wind grabbed us.

"We forgot to close the window earlier," I said, rushing to my bedroom.

My room was covered with snow! My bed, my shelves, my closet, and the carpet!

Everything was covered with a white blanket of heavy, cold snow. And there was more bad news. We had left our game on the floor while the wind blew through the open window.

It had scattered our trading cards all over my room. There were cards everywhere!

"We have to find the *nimbostratus* card and replace it with another one right now!" I screamed as I closed the window.

Lionel got down on his knees and started digging in the snow. It was as cold in the room as it had been outside. With our frozen hands, Lionel and I brushed piles of snow off my desk. Then we laid each card down.

We found soldiers, tanks, monsters, and a bunch of other characters and weapons. We were both shivering as we carefully placed each card on my desk to dry.

The snow melted. My bedroom floor quickly turned into a huge puddle.

Finally, Lionel yelled, "Yes! I found a *cirrostratus* card!"

He placed it in the middle of the room. We looked out the window. What would a *cirrostratus* card do?

Outside, the snow kept on falling, and the wind kept blowing.

I looked around and finally found another cloud card under my bed. I carefully put it on my desk. That didn't change the weather either.

Nothing happened when Lionel found a third cloud card, either. We were beginning to think it was no use.

Then I realized why the magic of the cloud cards was not working. It wouldn't work without the card that had started the snow in the first place.

"We have to find that *nimbostratus* card!" I cried. "The weather won't change until the old card is covered with a new card. The snow won't stop unless we find that card!"

"Oh, great," Lionel said.

We searched for over an hour. A hundred and fifty useless cards were piled on my desk.

My bedroom looked like it had been through a blizzard. I guess it really had been!

Lionel and I had torn my room apart, but we still hadn't found the one card we needed!

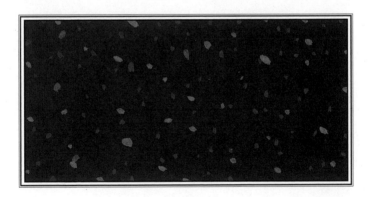

Chapter 5

THE STRANGER

"Stupid snow," I said, looking out my window.

The snowflakes were still piling up in the streets. The wind was blowing the snow against the houses and covering up parked cars.

No one was outside. It was too cold for that.

Lionel and I had looked through our pile of cards at least ten times. The card that started the snow must have been blown away through the open window while we were outside.

The card had to be out there, drowned under the white piles of snow that covered the neighborhood. We wouldn't be able to find it until the snow stopped and melted.

But for the snow to stop and the wind to calm down, we had to break the spell. And we couldn't break the spell without the card!

It was past midnight and we were desperate. Lionel and I looked out the window. We felt like criminals. The disaster was our fault, and we had no way to stop it.

Then a strange voice said, "So, are you proud of yourselves?"

Startled, we spun around. A tall man wearing a black raincoat was standing in my room.

How had he gotten into my apartment? And who was he?

He was waving something in his hand. It was the *nimbostratus* card!

"Did you, by any chance, play with this?" he asked.

"You found it!" I shouted at him.

The man grinned. He said, "Yes, I found it outside in the snow. Where are the other cards that I foolishly gave to your friend Gavin?"

"On my desk," I answered, confused.

The man went over to my desk. He picked up the pile of cards and started to look through them. One by one, he pulled out the other cloud cards.

The man gathered his eight cards and turned to us. "I made these cards to amuse my little neighbor, Gavin," he told us.

"I have known him since he was a baby," he went on. "The only thing is, I used the wrong materials."

I was confused. "What do you mean?" I asked.

"Masters of the weather can sometimes make mistakes," he said, winking at me. "I used the wrong kind of ink. These little cards have become way too powerful! They're too dangerous!"

"We have to stop that storm!" Lionel said.

"That's why I'm here," the man said.

He held up the eight cloud cards. He took a deep breath, and then blew on the cards.

Suddenly, they all burst into flames!

Just before the flames reached his fingers, the man dropped the burning pieces on the floor.

"Now, look outside," the man commanded.

Lionel and I did what we were told.

The moon and the stars were showing in the sky. The clouds were blowing away.

And the snow had stopped. It was finally over.

"In a day or two, everything will be melted," the stranger said.

Then he pulled another card from the pocket of his raincoat. It wasn't one of the special cloud cards.

"I'm keeping this one," he told us. "It's the invisibility card that Gavin traded me. I changed this one a little bit too. It helped me find you and get into your apartment. Good night, gentlemen! And don't forget: The weather is not a game."

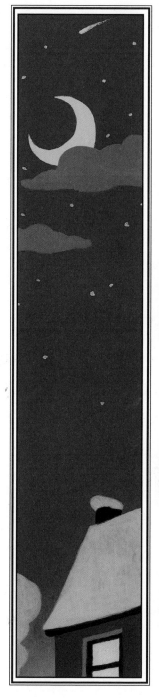

Then, as quickly as he had arrived, the man disappeared.

Lionel and I stared at each other. Then we got a bucket and some rags. We had to clean up my room before my mom got home.

"We should have asked that guy for a card that would help us clean everything up," grumbled Lionel.

I smiled. "Or a trick to get us out of trouble when my mom comes home and sees this mess!" I said. "But even the world's greatest magician wouldn't be able to help us with that," I added.

"Really?" Lionel asked. "That guy could move clouds, weather, and storms. Don't you think he could do something?"

I shook my head.

I told Lionel, "You know what happens when my mom gets mad. Talk about a storm!"

THE END

ABOUT THE AUTHOR

Hubert Ben Kemoun was born in 1958 in
Algeria, on the northern coast of Africa. He
has written plays for radio, screenplays for
television, musicals for the stage, and children's
books. He now lives in Nantes, France with his
wife and their two sons, Nicolas and Nathan.
He likes writing detective stories, and also creates
crossword puzzles for newspapers. When he
writes stories, he writes them first with a pen
and then types the words on a computer.
His favorite color is black, the color of ink.

ABOUT THE ILLUSTRATOR

Thomas Ehretsmann was born in 1974 on the
eastern border of France in the town of Mulhouse
(pronounced mee-yoo-looz). He created his
own comic strips at the age of 6, inspired by
the newspapers his father read. Ehretsmann
studied decorative arts in the ancient cathedral
town of Strassbourg, and worked with a world-
famous publisher of graphic novels, Delcourt
Editions. Ehretsmann now works primarily as an
illustrator of books for adults and children.

Glossary

battle (BAT-uhl)—a fight between two armies

coincidence (koh-IN-si-duhnss)—a chance happening

desperate (DESS-pur-it)—if you are desperate, you will do anything to change your situation

invisibility (in-viz-uh-BIL-ih-tee)—in this book, an invisibility card made the person who had it unable to be seen

master (MASS-tur)—a person with power

musketeer (muss-kih-TEER)—a soldier armed with a gun called a musket

neighbor (NAY-bur)—someone who lives nearby

numb (NUHM)—unable to feel anything

soldier (SOLE-jur)—someone in the army

strange (STRAYNJ)—different from the usual, unfamiliar

weapon (WEP-uhn)—something that can be used in a fight to attack or defend

CLOUDS . . .

Clouds have been around for millions of years, but their names haven't. Luke Howard, a British chemist who was born in 1772, invented cloud names. When he was 30 years old, he published a scientific paper giving the names that we now use to classify clouds.

Cirrus (SEER-us) comes from the Latin word meaning "a curl of hair." These wispy, curly clouds are the highest clouds, drifting over 16,000 feet above the earth's surface.

Stratus (STRAT-iss) means "layer." These clouds cover the sky like blankets. When low stratus clouds touch the ground, they are known as fog.

Big puffy or cottony clouds are called **cumulus** (KYOO-myuh-luss) clouds. Their name means "pile."

... THE REAL MASTERS OF WEATHER!

Howard also used the word **nimbus** (NIM-biss) to describe some clouds. The word simply means "rain."

For example, a **cumulonimbus** (KYOO-myuh-loh-NIM-buss) cloud is a big, puffy cloud that holds tons of water droplets. The water droplets fall to earth as rain.

Clouds come in various colors, depending on the amount of moisture in them, or how sunlight passes through them. They can be white, gray, blue, yellow, orange, red, or pink. Green clouds signify heavy rain, wind, hail, and possibly a tornado.

DISCUSSION QUESTIONS

1. In this book, Sam and Lionel meet a man who calls himself a Master of Weather. What do you think a Master of Weather does?

2. When Sam and Lionel start a blizzard, they go out and have a snowball fight. Then they build a snowman. What would you do in a blizzard? Talk about the things that you can do when it snows.

3. If you could control the weather, what would you do? What kind of weather would you choose? Why?

WRITING PROMPTS

1. The man that Lionel and Sam meet says that he used an invisibility card to enter Sam's apartment. What would you do if you had a card that could make you invisible?

2. On a piece of paper, draw a cloud. Make up a name for it. What does the cloud do? Draw your own cloud card, like the cards in this book. Don't forget to include a description of what the cloud's power is.

3. Sam and Lionel love playing with their Terror Universe cards. What is your favorite thing to do with your best friend? Write about it.

Internet Sites

Do you want to know more about subjects related to this book? Or are you interested in learning about other topics? Then check out FactHound, a fun, easy way to find Internet sites.

Our investigative staff has already sniffed out great sites for you!

Here's how to use FactHound:

1. Visit *www.facthound.com*

2. Select your grade level.

3. To learn more about subjects related to this book, type in the book's ISBN number: **9781434204790**.

4. Click the **Fetch It** button.

FactHound will fetch the best Internet sites for you!